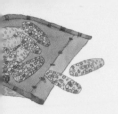

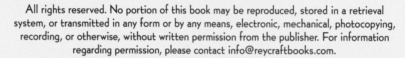
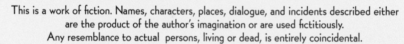
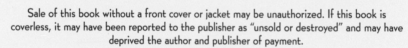

Reycraft Books
55 Fifth Avenue
New York, NY 10003

Reycraftbooks.com

Reycraft Books is a trade imprint and trademark of Newmark Learning, LLC.

This edition is published by arrangement with
China Children's Press & Publication Group, China.
© China Children's Press & Publication Group

Library of Congress Cataloging-in-Publication Data is available.

ISBN: 978-1-4788-6934-4

Printed in Guangzhou, China. 4401/0120/CA22000002

10 9 8 7 6 5 4 3 2 1

First Edition Hardcover published by Reycraft Books 2020

REYCRAFT
BOOKS

Sweet Laba Congee

By Qiusheng Zhang • Illustrated by Chengliang Zhu

My name is Yan'er.

Our house is at the east
end of the village,
in a valley.

Our neighbors' homes are called
the Zhang Family Compound,
the Li Family Compound,
and the Zhao Family Compound,
while our home is called the
Red Persimmon Compound
because of the big persimmon
tree in our yard.

According to tradition, every family cooks laba congee during the Laba Festival on the eighth day of the twelfth month of the lunar calendar.

The day before the festival this year, Grandma and I sat under the persimmon tree, organizing the ingredients for this tasty porridge.

We prepared a wide
variety of ingredients,
such as rice, sorghum, corn, millet, and

chestnuts, walnuts, and dates.

It was a lot of work to gather and clean all the ingredients.

On the morning of the Laba Festival, I woke up to
the familiar smell of the congee. Rolling out of bed,
I ran to the kitchen and helped Mom add firewood
to the wood-burning stove.

We had a gas stove at home.

But Grandma insisted on using

the wood-burning stove and a

large pot for making the

laba congee because this

was the only way to

guarantee *it would be perfect.*

When the laba congee began to boil, the smell attracted our puppy, who circled around the kitchen stove.

The congee was ready around noon. But it was not time to eat yet. Grandma filled bowls with congee and worshipped our ancestors and gods with them. Grandma asked the ancestors and gods for favorable weather in the coming year and a good harvest.

She also asked for family peace and prosperity, especially for my dad, who was working in a different city, and my uncle, who was studying at a university.

The next job was mine.

Carrying the pot with the laba congee in it, I delivered some to the oldest men and women in our village.

Back home our yard was warm, bathed in the noon sunshine. My family sat under the persimmon tree and ate the laba congee, which was shared by our puppy and the birds in the tree.

Some congee was left in the pot. Grandma said that we
would save it for Dad and Uncle. I knew they were coming
back because the Spring Festival was drawing near.

Grandma gave me half
a bowl to smear on
the tree in the yard.

According to a legend,

this will help the tree grow
better and produce more
persimmons next year.

It began to snow
right after the
Laba Festival.

Watching the snowflakes fall, my friends and

played on the hillside, singing,

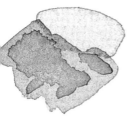

"Stop crying, dear little one.
    After laba, you'll get pork.
Stop crying, dear little one.
    A new year is coming soon."